ABOUT PIXAR ANIMATION STUDIOS
ARTIST SHOWCASE BOOKS

This series of original picture books puts the spotlight on the

incredible artists of Pixar Animation Studios. The pages of each

book showcase the personal work of one of these talented artists

and introduce a brand-new world and characters.

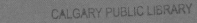

PIXAR ANIMATION STUDIOS ARTIST SHOWCASE

HENRI'S *Hats*

Mike Wu

Disney • Press
Los Angeles • New York

Today Mama has surprised me.
She says we are going on an adventure
far away from the lights and sounds of the city,
so I have brought my own lights and sounds.

We've come to see my Grand-Papa, who I call Papa for short. I haven't seen him since I was small. I study Papa carefully and think about what Mama has told me.

She told me three things
about Papa.

He is old.
He is quiet.
He is a little bit shy.

Papa's dog, George, is not one bit old
or quiet, and he is especially not shy.
He takes my hat and runs!

I run fast, but George runs faster ...

past the clock and up the stairs ...

. . . right to an old and dusty trunk.
I feel a patter in my chest and a twinkle
in my toes. I wonder what the trunk is
hiding. It isn't treasure or gold but . . .

lots and lots of
hats!

I put on a helmet and imagine
I'm in the Grand Prix,
speeding my way to the finish line!

With a change of hat,
I'm sailing into the sunset,
my first mate at the prow!

Ahoy!

But there is still more
adventure to be had.

I explore the deep ocean
and escape with all my toes!

Hello,
Mr. Shark!

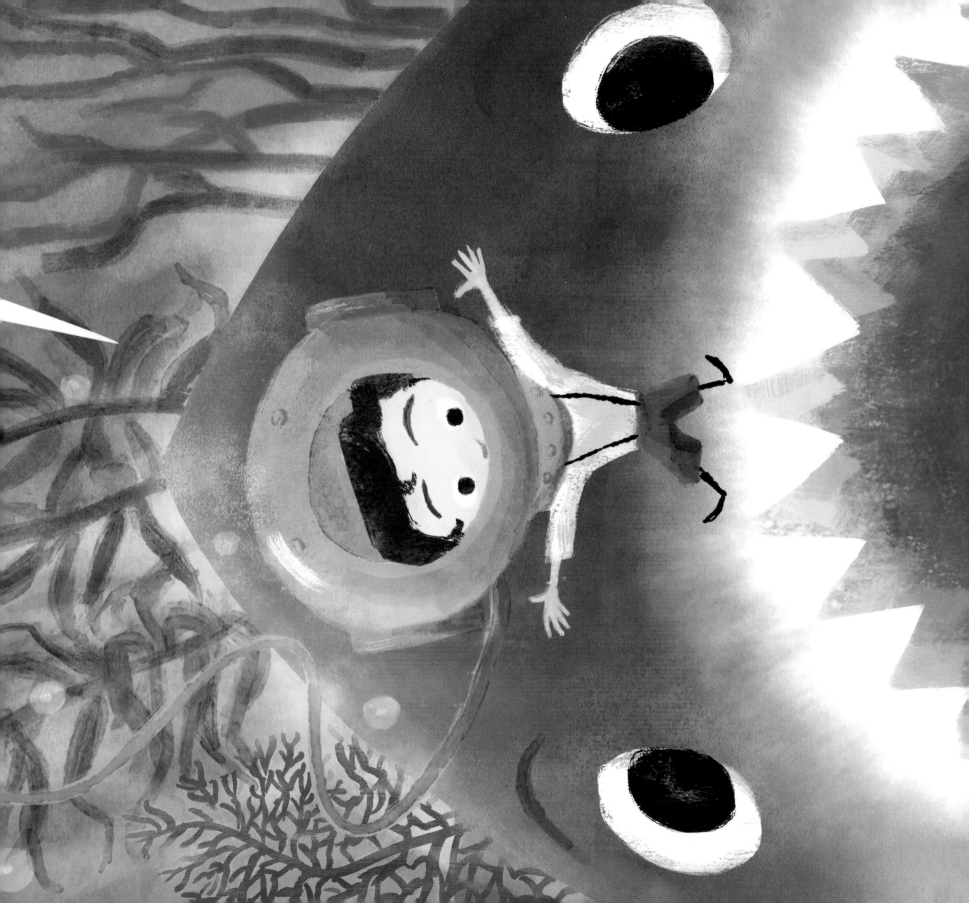

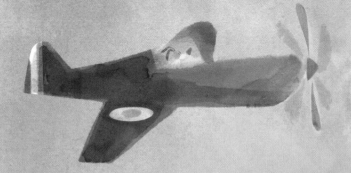

I soar beside the clouds through dangerous skies.
Watch out, George!

> > > > >

At first, I worry Papa might be angry.
Instead, he takes the ringmaster hat
and puts it on his head.

He pulls back the curtain
and reveals . . .

…that he has gone on many adventures!
Papa tells me that he has been a
race car driver,

a ship's captain,

and a scuba diver,

and he once worked in a
circus,
long, long ago.

I realize now that we are not so different,
Papa and I, except most of his adventures
are behind him, and mine are still ahead.

Papa gives me a present and tells me there's one adventure he still dreams about.

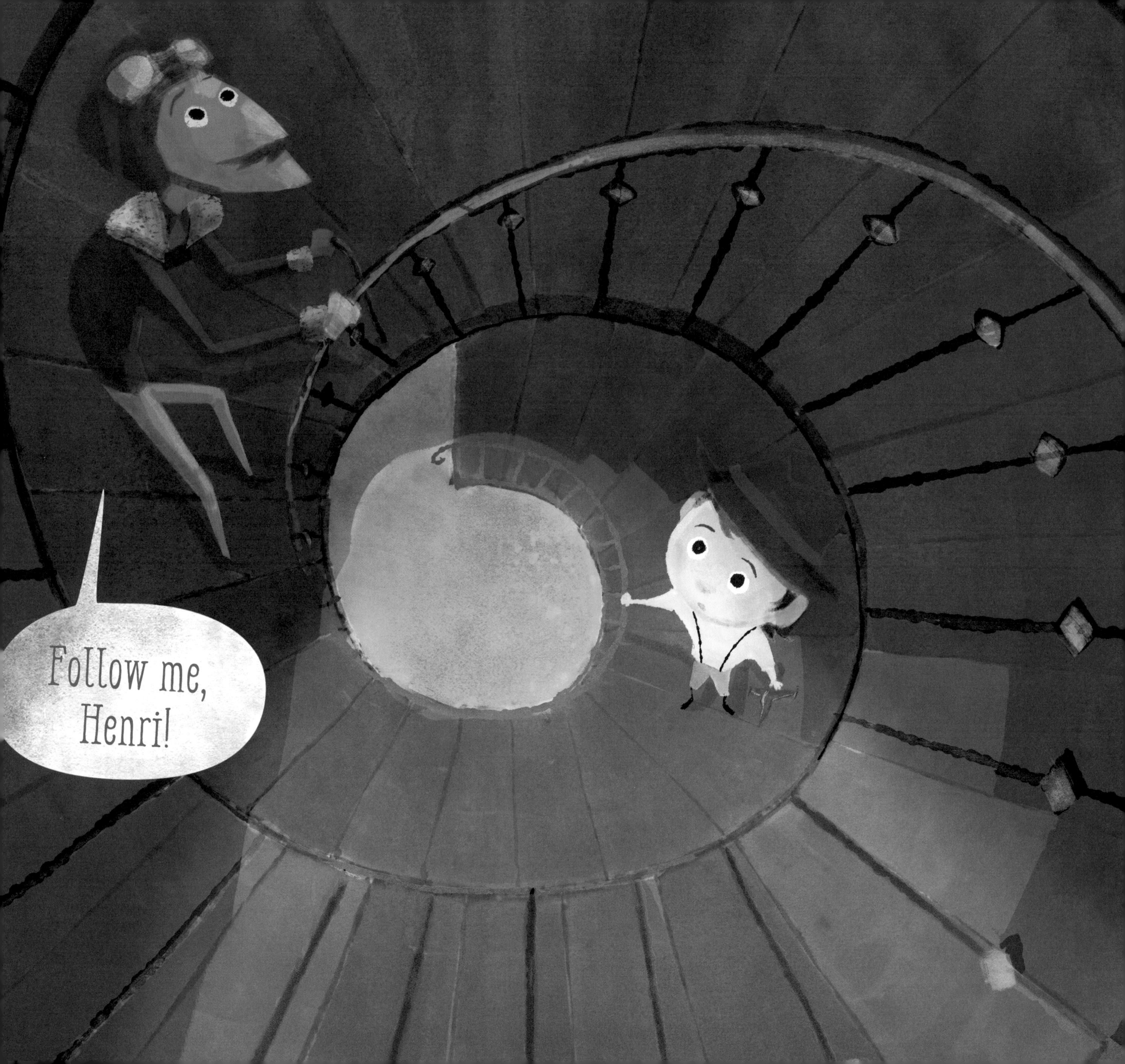
Follow me, Henri!

Papa never made it to the moon, but he says maybe that can be my adventure.

Someday I hope to be like Papa,
with a trunk full of hats and
a life full of adventure.

Author's Note

Hi! I'm Mike, but my friends call me Wu or Wudog.
As a kid, I loved to draw and create art. By the ripe old age of seven,
I already knew I wanted a career in animation. I watched *Luxo Jr.*
and I was hooked! I wanted to work somewhere I could live out
my dream of helping create movies.

Like Papa in *Henri's Hats*, my immigrant dad wore many
different hats. While wearing his business hat, he owned a restaurant
in New York in Chinatown, where I would go nearly every day to eat.
It was so good! All the tastes, sounds, and sights of the city inspired me.

I attended CalArts, and that's how I got my start in animation.
First I worked at Walt Disney Feature Animation, on classic films such as
Hercules, *Mulan*, and *Tarzan*. Now I work at Pixar Animation Studios,
and I've helped create *The Incredibles*, *Ratatouille*, *Up*,
Toy Story 3, and *Coco*.

CalArts gave me a love for watercolor painting, which led me
to become an author and illustrator of picture books. I'm particularly proud
of *Henri's Hats*, as it was my very first picture book idea. Since then,
I've created the popular Ellie series and illustrated
the Oodlethunks chapter book series.

Believe it or not, I wear many other hats, too!
I'm a small-business entrepreneur, a home chef, a husband,
and a dad to two children. I hope *Henri's Hats* will inspire you
to embrace a life of adventure, which starts with a
grand imagination and maybe a couple of hats.

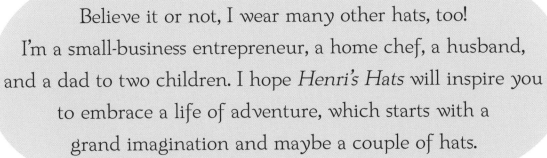

First Hardcover Edition, September 2018

1 3 5 7 9 10 8 6 4 2

FAC-029191-18138

ISBN 978-1-4847-0903-0

Printed in Malaysia

This book is set in Packard Patrician.

Designed by Mike Wu and Scott Piehl.

Illustrations created with digital brushes.

Library of Congress Cataloging-in-Publication Data

Names: Wu, Mike, author, illustrator.

Title: Henri's hats / Mike Wu.

Description: First edition. Los Angeles ; New York : Disney Press, 2018.

Series: Pixar Animation Studios artist showcase

Summary: A trunk filled with amazing hats shows Henri that his grandfather is not just a quiet old man,

but someone who once had the sort of grand adventures Henri imagines.

Identifiers: LCCN 2017060928 ISBN 9781484709030 (hardcover)

Subjects: CYAC: Adventure and adventurers–Fiction. Hats–Fiction.

Grandfathers–Fiction. Imagination–Fiction.

Classification: LCC PZ7.W96225 Hen 2018 DDC [E]–dc23

LC record available at https://lccn.loc.gov/2017060928

Reinforced binding

Visit www.disneybooks.com

For Baba and the real Papa

–M.W.

Fin